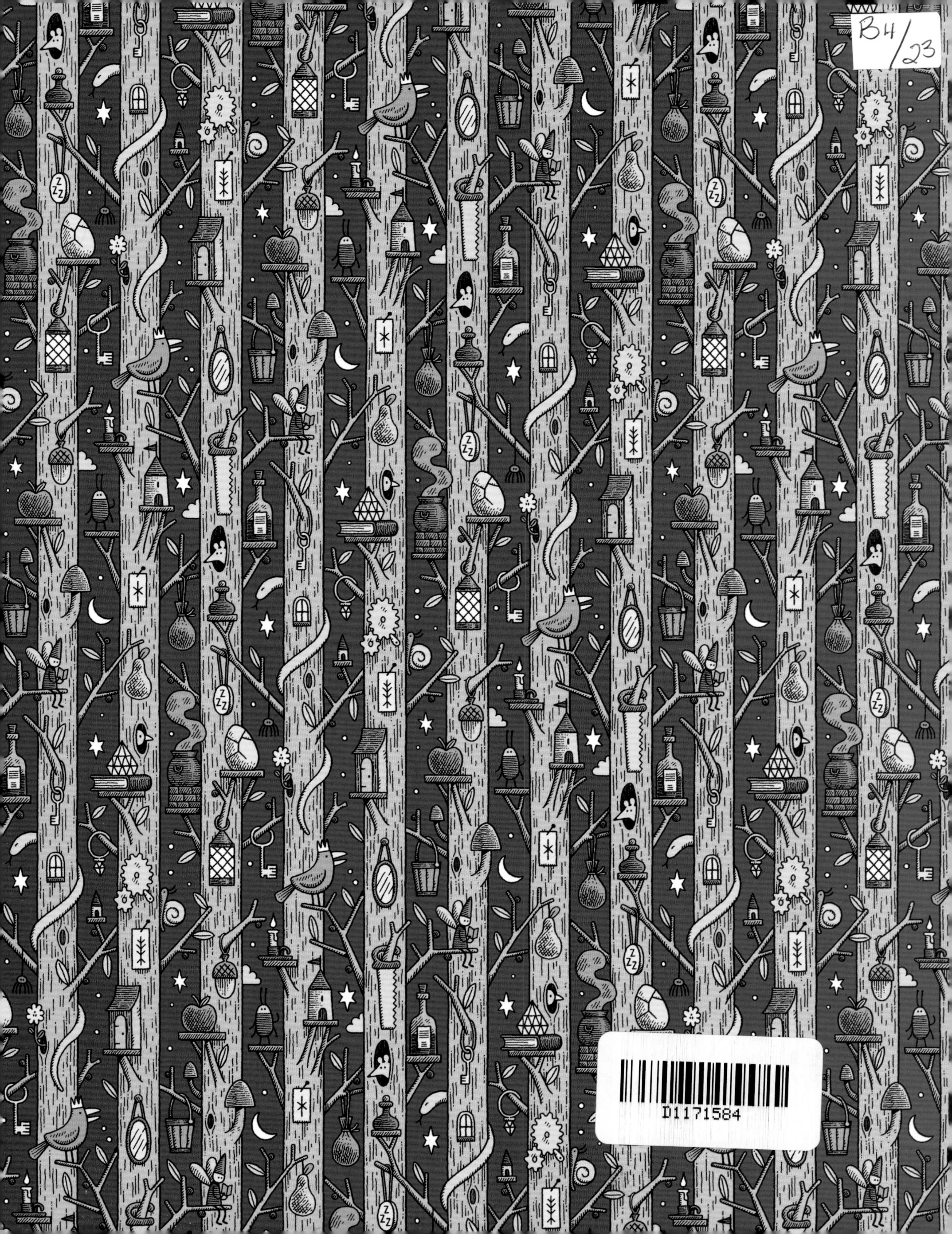

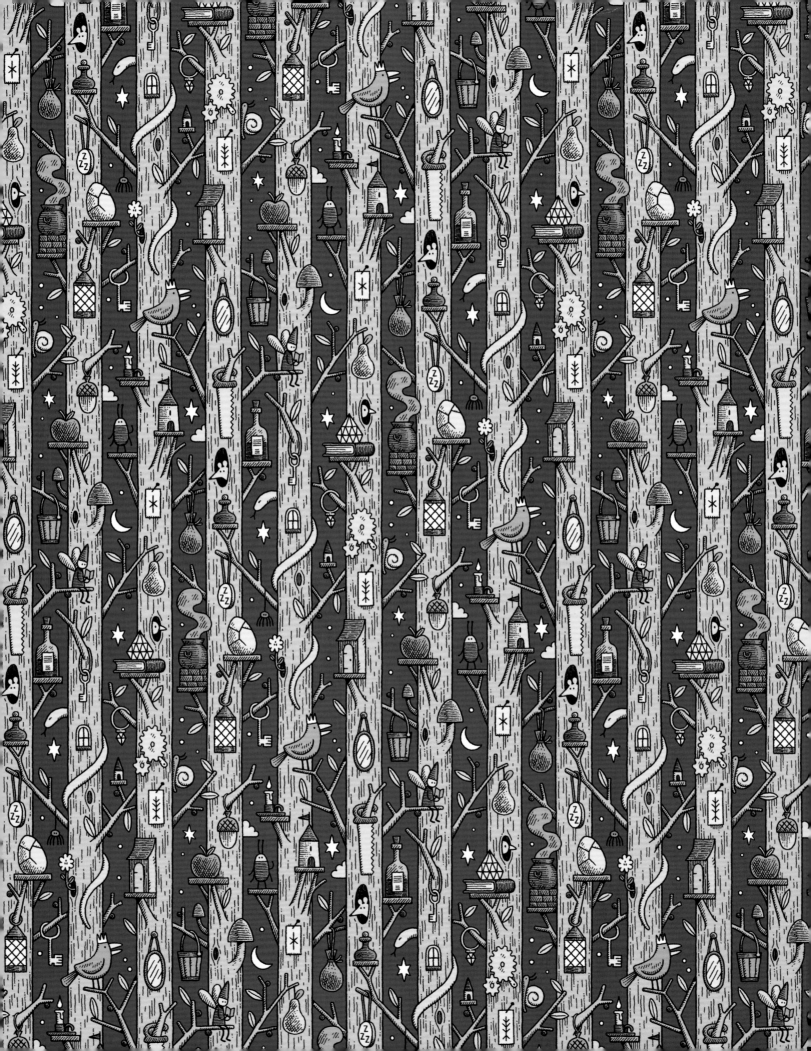

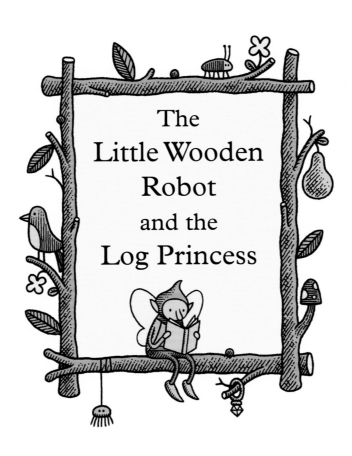

The
Little Wooden
Robot
and the
Log Princess

For Ben and Jack

Thank you to Matthew Forsythe, Daphne Gauld,
Iris Gauld, Billy Kiosoglou, and Jo Taylor.

Neal Porter Books

Text copyright and illustration copyright © 2021 by Tom Gauld
All Rights Reserved
HOLIDAY HOUSE is registered in the U.S. Patent and Trademark Office.
Printed and bound in June 2022 at C&C Offset in Shenzhen, China.
The artwork for this book was created with with pen on paper
for the drawings and a computer for the color.
www.holidayhouse.com
First Edition
5   7   9   10   8   6

Library of Congress Cataloging-in-Publication Data

Names: Gauld, Tom, author, illustrator.
Title: The little wooden robot and the log princess / by Tom Gauld.
Description: First edition. | New York : Holiday House, 2021. | "A Neal
Porter book." | Audience: Ages 4 to 8. | Audience: Grades K–1. |
Summary: When a wooden robot prince forgets to say the magic words that
turn his sister from a log into a princess she is thrown away, so he
goes on an epic journey to find her and bring her back.
Identifiers: LCCN 2020025839 | ISBN 9780823446988 (hardcover)
Subjects: CYAC: Fairy tales. | Brothers and sisters—Fiction. |
Robots—Fiction.
Classification: LCC PZ8.G286 Li 2021 | DDC [E]—dc23
LC record available at https://lccn.loc.gov/2020025839

ISBN: 978-0-8234-4698-8 (hardcover)

The LITTLE WOODEN ROBOT and the LOG PRINCESS

TOM GAULD

NEAL PORTER BOOKS
HOLIDAY HOUSE / NEW YORK

There once lived a king and queen
who happily ruled a pleasant land,
but they had no children.

So one night the king went to see the royal
inventor, and the queen went to see a
clever old witch who lived in the woods.

They both asked for the same thing: a child.

The inventor set to work straight away. She used her finest tools and her most ingenious designs and she built a wonderful, intricate little wooden robot.

The witch took a log from the basket by her fire
and used her deepest magic to bring the wood to life
in the form of a perfect little log princess.

The king and the queen and the princess
and the robot all loved each other instantly.

The log princess was bold and clever,
but she had a secret: each night when she fell asleep,
she turned back into a log and would stay like that
until she was woken by the magic words
"Awake, little log, awake."

The little wooden robot was brave and kind.
So kind, in fact, that he let a family of beetles nest
in his workings, even though it tickled sometimes.

Every day, the robot would wake his log-sister and they
would play in the castle and the gardens until the sun
went down and they were tired out.

However, one morning, a traveling circus came to visit and the robot rushed down to the courtyard without waking his sister. On the stairs he passed a maid going up to tidy the princess's bedroom.

When the maid saw the log she said, "Oh dear! A plain old log, lying in the princess's bed! What a disgrace!" And threw it out of the window.

At that very moment the little robot thought of his sister.

"How selfish of me!" he said to himself. "She's missing out on all these wonderful things." And he ran to her bedroom to wake her up.

He looked at the empty bed in horror. "Where's the log?" he cried.

"Oh, *that*," said the maid. "I threw it out of the window."

The robot looked out and spied the
log rolling across the courtyard.

He raced down, but the castle was atop a steep hill,
and the log had rolled through the gate, over the
drawbridge, and down toward the village.

A goblin was pushing a barrow of logs through the village and the princess-log rolled right up to him.

"What a lucky day!" he said. "Another fine log for my load."

The goblin took the logs to the river, where a barge was tied up. The captain paid him a copper coin and his barrow-load was tipped into the barge with hundreds and hundreds of other logs.

The robot ran to the barge. "Please, sir," he said to the captain. "My special log is in your barge. May I come aboard and search for it?"

"You may," said the captain. "But we must set sail straight away, while the wind is right."

So the robot clambered on, and the barge set off for the frozen North. They sailed for days, but there were so very many logs that, even with the help of the crew, the little wooden robot could not find the right one.

They arrived and unloaded the cargo.
"Come back with us," said the captain. "The North is
a dangerous place and we can easily find you
another log when we get home."

"I can't," said the robot. "That log is the most precious
thing in the world to me. I won't leave without it."

So the crew gave him a map, some supplies, and a handcart and sailed back to the pleasant land where our story began.

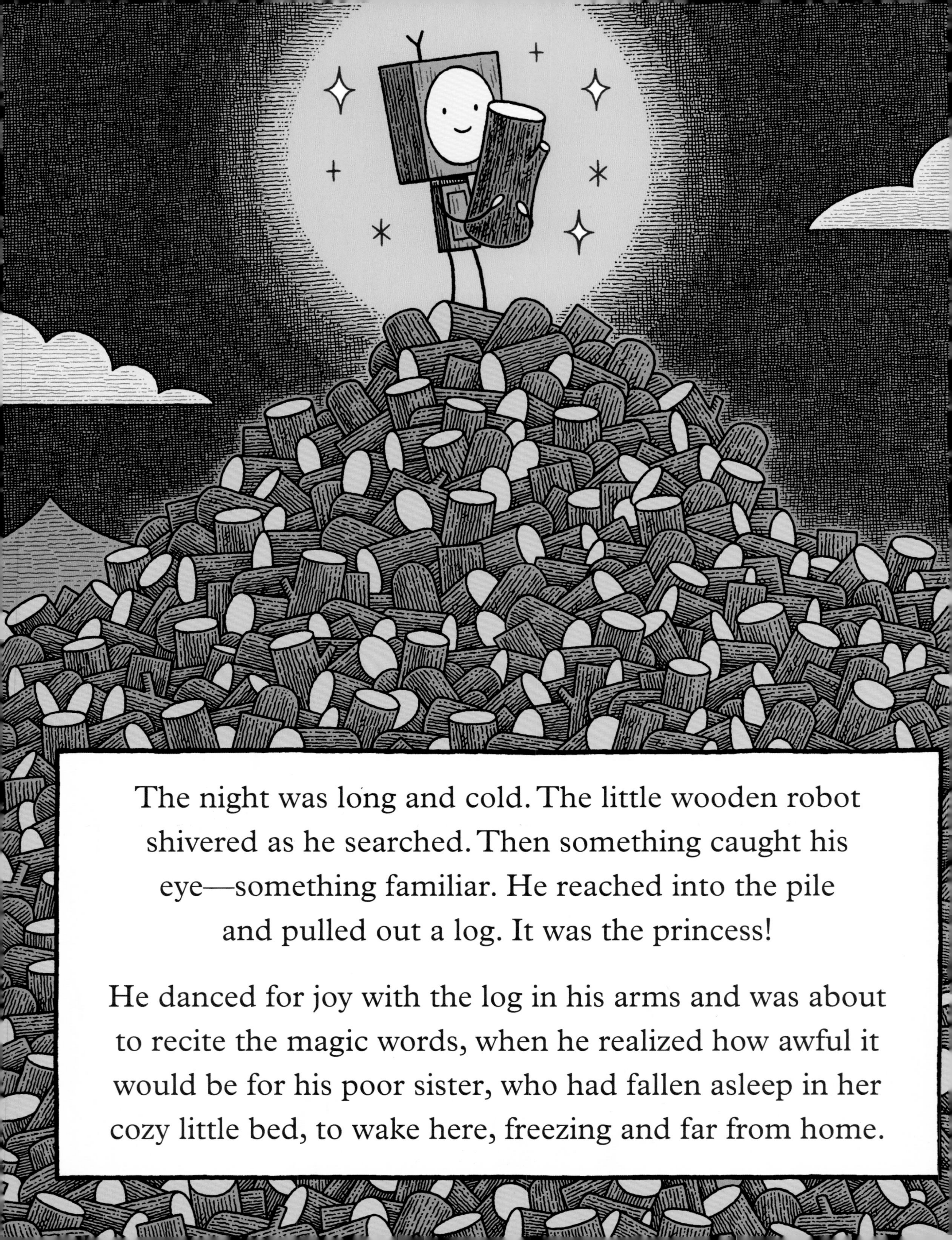

The night was long and cold. The little wooden robot shivered as he searched. Then something caught his eye—something familiar. He reached into the pile and pulled out a log. It was the princess!

He danced for joy with the log in his arms and was about to recite the magic words, when he realized how awful it would be for his poor sister, who had fallen asleep in her cozy little bed, to wake here, freezing and far from home.

So he put her into the handcart, tucked a blanket around her, took up the handle, and began the long walk home.

Along the way he had too many adventures
to recount here:

The
Giant's Key

The Family
of Robbers

The Old Lady
in a Bottle

The Magic
Pudding

The Lonely
Bear

The Queen of
the Mushrooms

But each left him more exhausted than the last: his joints became stiff and his cogs and gears wore down, until one day he could go no further.

With the last of his strength he said the magic words,
woke the princess and told her what had happened,
how it was all his fault, and that he understood that
she would probably never forgive him.

"Oh, Brother," she said, "how silly of you to keep all
these worries to yourself. Of course I forgive you!"
She helped him into the handcart, where he fell
into a deep sleep. She took the map and the handle
of the cart and continued the walk home.

She too had many adventures:

The Mischievous
Pixies

The
Dragon's Egg

The Feuding
Hunters

The
Haunted Well

The Enormous
Blackbird

The Baby in
a Rosebush

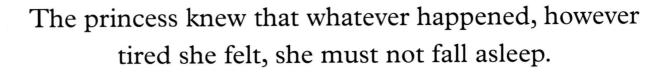

The princess knew that whatever happened, however tired she felt, she must not fall asleep.

But one night, as she was trudging through a dark forest—which she was sure couldn't be *that* far from home—she began to yawn. And then she yawned some more. And her eyes felt heavy. And her legs felt tired. And she thought of her cozy little bed in the castle.

"Perhaps I shall close my eyes, just for a moment," she said. And with that, she fell asleep and—pop!—turned into a log.

The king and queen missed their children terribly.
Soldiers had been sent searching in every direction and
a huge reward had been offered, but it was no good.

The queen would not leave her bed and the king sat
alone in a tower, staring out at the deep, dark forest.

Little did he know that in the forest was a clearing, and in that clearing was a handcart, and in the handcart was a little wooden robot, and in that robot's worn-out, broken-down workings, a family of beetles was wondering why everything was so still and so quiet.

They climbed out and looked at the log and the robot and knew that they must do something.

So they stopped a passing mouse and asked her for help, and she asked a bird, who asked a rabbit, who asked a fox. And they all worked together to take the princess and the robot to the nearest house: the home of a clever old witch.

The witch recognized the pair immediately.

She woke the princess, repaired the robot, and set off for the castle.

The king could hardly believe his eyes as he watched the little group, all crowded onto a broomstick, fly over the forest and set down in the castle courtyard.

The robot and the princess and
the queen and the king all hugged
and laughed and cried.

The witch was thanked, the month was declared a holiday for the whole kingdom, the beetles were each given a tiny golden medal,

and they all lived happily ever after.

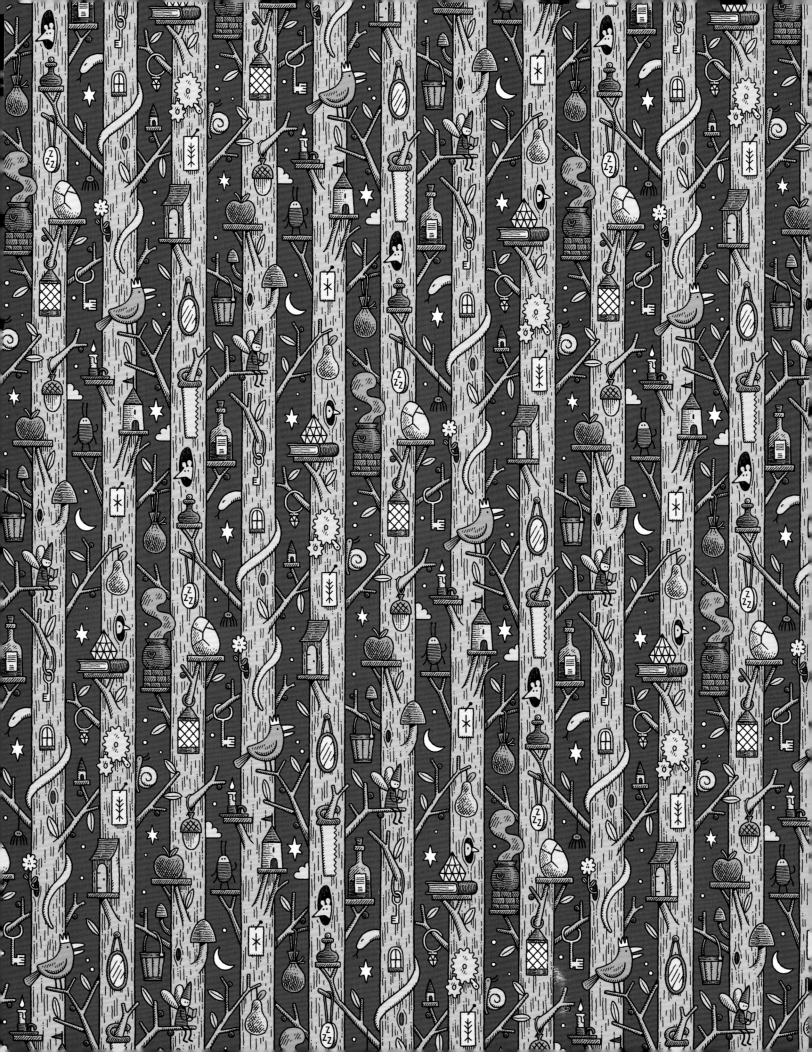

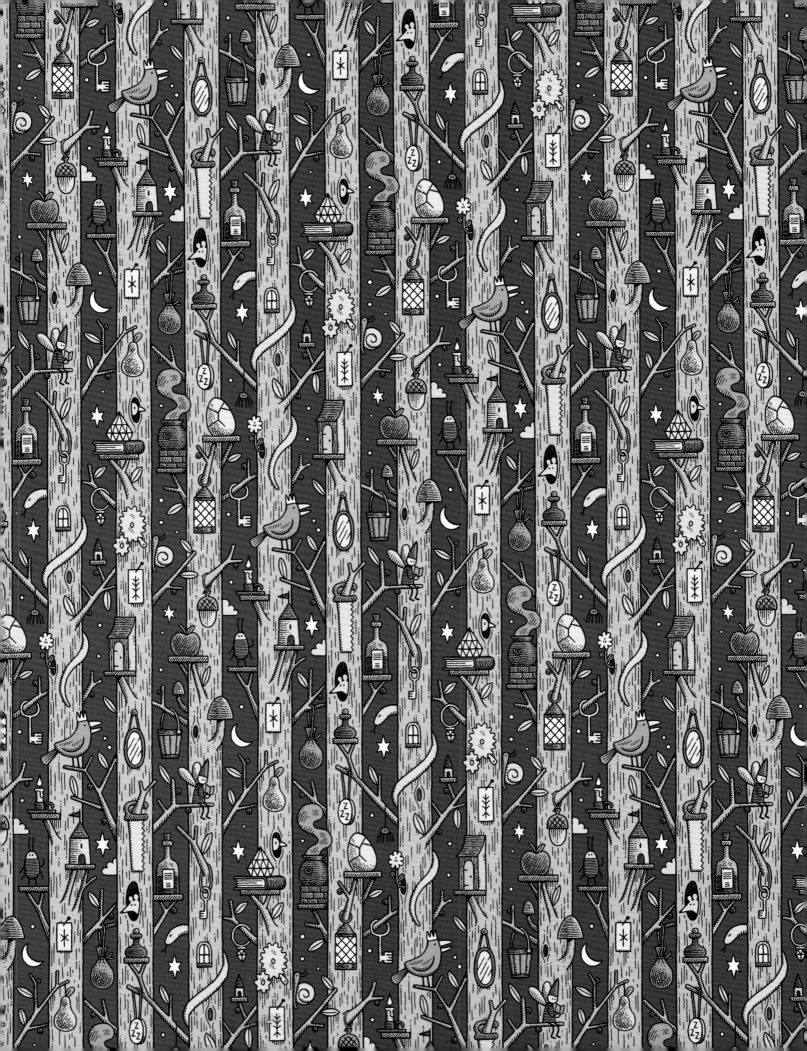